AF225582

The Goblins' Christmas

by Elizabeth Anderson

Copyright © 10/23/2015
Jefferson Publication

ISBN-13: 978-1518748714

Printed in the United States of America

ONCE upon a time I visited Fairy-land and spent a day in Goblin-town. The people there are much like ourselves, only they are very, very small and roguish. They play pranks on one another and have great fun. They are good natured and jolly, and rarely get angry. But if one does get angry, he quickly recovers his good nature and joins again in the sport.

If a Goblin should continue angry he would take on some visible form. Perhaps he would become a toad or a squirrel, or some other little animal, and would have to live here on the Earth-plane forevermore. But, if he keeps good natured, he can come here and have his fun, and not be seen by any one except a Seer, or very wise person.

The Goblins are gracious to the wise people now, but they were not always so. A long, long time ago, on a Christmas-eve, the Fairy-folk were having great sport. All the little people of the Unseen-world had gathered together in the Earth-realm. There were Brownies, and Gnomes, and Elves;

even some little Cherubs had joined them. They were having a wild dance and a gay time when who should appear but Kris Kringle! Now the Fairies did not know that he was a Magician, or Seer, and so they tried to make sport of him. But Kris by his wonderful magic, changed them into the most beautiful toys. They became straight little jumping-jacks, and dolls in bright dresses, and the dearest little rabbit with white, soft fur. And somewhere in the bottom of the sleigh one was turned into a cute little Teddy-bear. Then old Kris tucked all these toys into his roomy sleigh, and shook the reins of his waiting steed. "Go on!" he said, "For I've many, many a chimney to reach tonight."

Now this is the tale of "The Goblins' Christmas" that the moonbeams told, as they heard it from the Fairy-Queen, who declares that every word of it is perfectly true.

HE little Man, and tiny Maid, Who love the Fairies in the glade, Who see them in the tangled grass The Gnomes and Brownies, as they pass, Who hear the Sprites from Elf-land call Go, frolic with these Brownies small, And join these merry sporting Elves, But ever be your own sweet selves.

The big bright Moon hung high and round, In a densely darkened sky; The tall pines swayed, and mocked, and groaned; The mountains grew so high That the Man-in-the-Moon came out and said, "Ho! Spooks, for a merry dance." The winds blow hard, the caverns roar, While o'er the earth they prance.

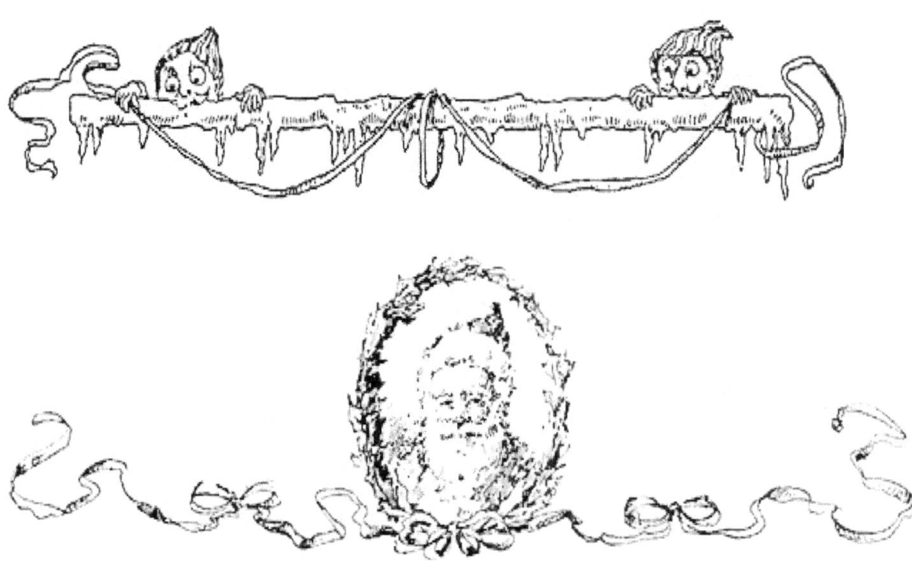

A Witch and a Goblin led the sprites; Out from the sky they sprung; And down the milky way they slid, And over

a chasm swung. The streams around ran witches' broth,
The fumes were strong and rank. These Elfin creatures
all were wroth, While of the stuff they drank.

The cunning Moon looked on and laughed With a shrill
and sneering jibe; Her soul grew fat to see them chaffed,
This mad and elfish tribe. The big black caldron boiled so
high With food for these queer mites, That it lit the

world throughout the sky, And down came all the Sprites.

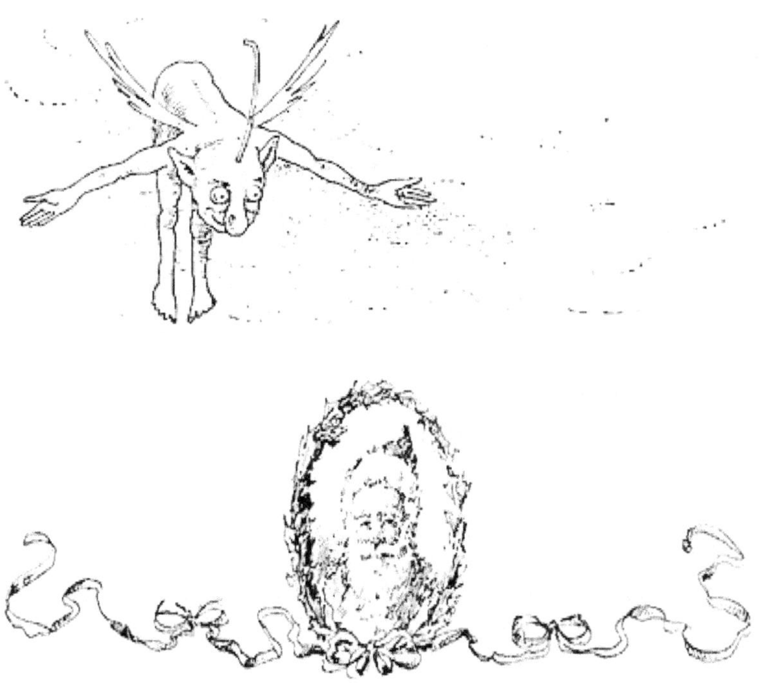

Their mad career upset a star, As through the air they flew: It cringed in fear, and shot afar, And fell where no one knew. Orion's sword was broke in bits, Corona's crown was gone, Capella seemed to lose her wits, While all so longed for dawn.

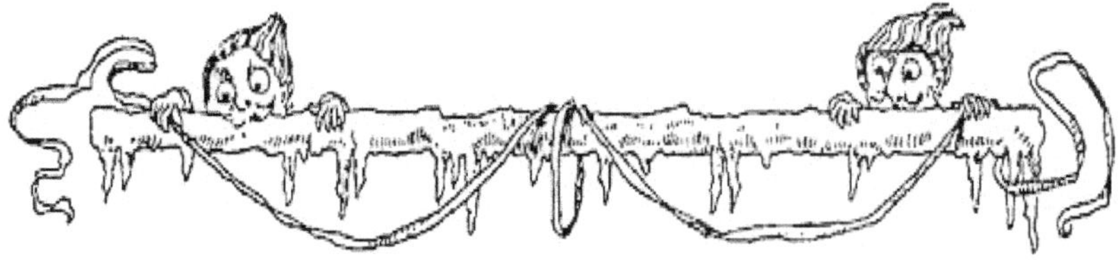

Then from the night there came a sound Of sleigh-bells ringing sweet; Out of the chaos came a man— Kris Kringle—for his Christmas treat. "Ho! Kris!" they cried, "We'll have some fun, We'll bind the old man down, We'll tie him up, and toss him o'er Into our Goblin-town."

They climbed the sleigh with shout and din, To bind his hands and feet; A hundred strong they clambered in Our good old Kris to meet. He sat quite still, with twinkling eyes, Then seized his mystic wand, He raised it up, and waved it round Stilled was this chattering band.

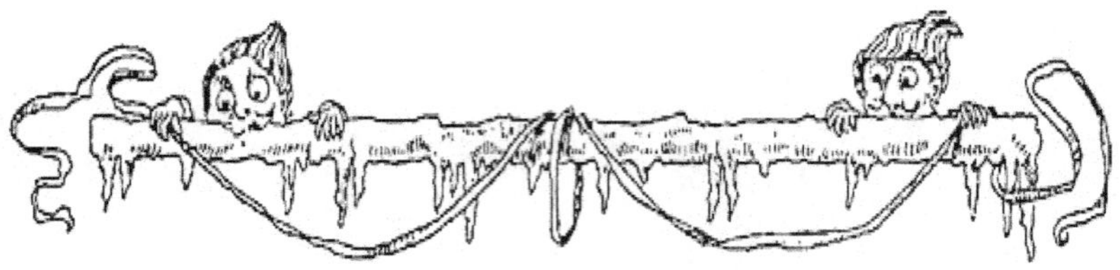

Stiffly stark and still they stood, Clad in elfish clothes;
Some were wax, and some were wood, One had crushed
his nose. "Playthings rare," he said and smiled, "For
children rich and poor; Some I'll leave the crippled child,
And some at the orphan's door."

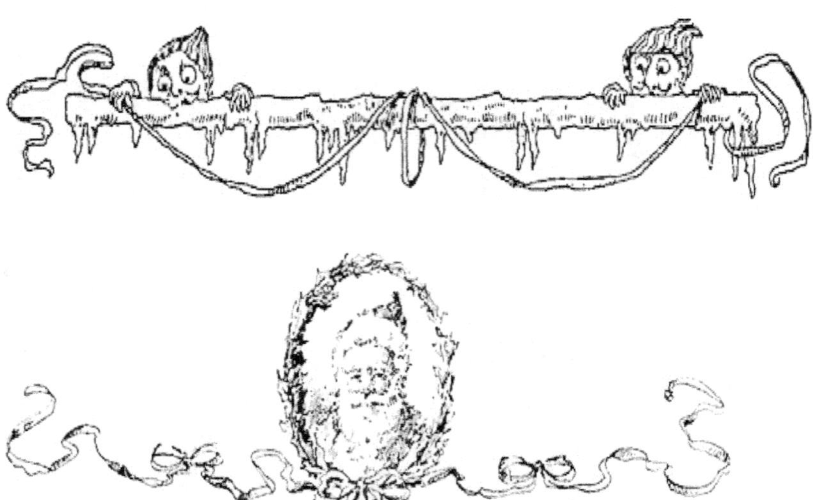

He shook his reins, and called his steed To bear him swiftly on. Full well it knew its Master's need To hurry e'er the dawn. From house to house they scampered down, Their sleigh-bells ringing clear, Through chimneys in the sleepy town— Good Kris and his reindeer.

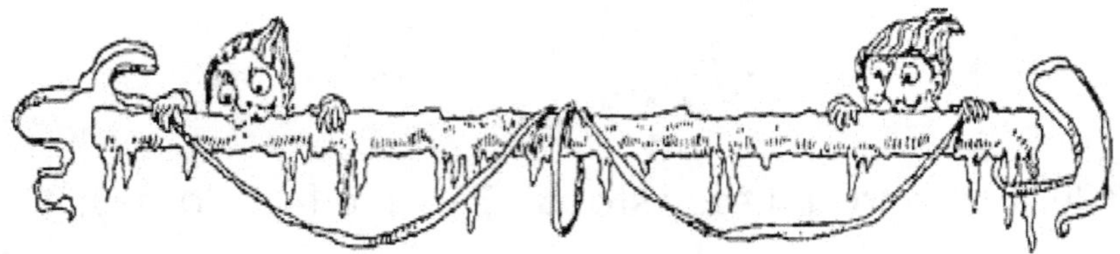

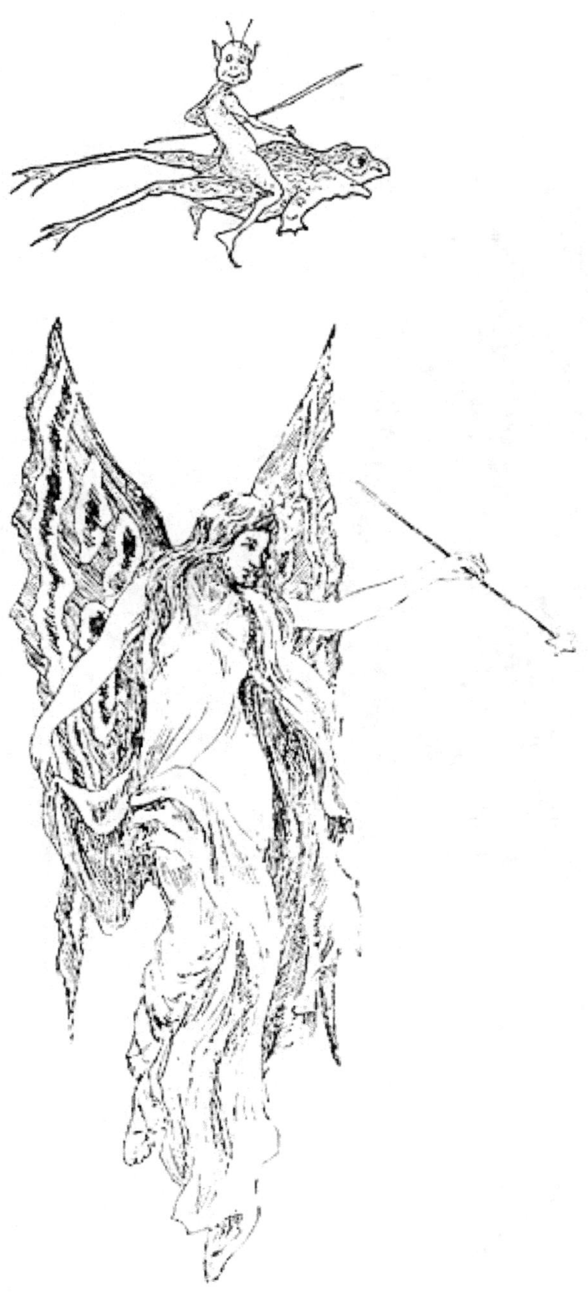

The windows rattled, the moonbeams tattled A tale so strange and queer. They told how at night, in dire affright The Moon had hid in fear.

That he'd called in sport his elfish court Of spooks and witches gay, Each Elfin child, by glee beguiled, Brought scores of others, they say.

Then a man appeared, with flowing beard, In a sled with a reindeer fleet; They gathered about with din and shout, To bind him hands and feet.

Then the Moon laughed loud at the gathering crowd, While he held his sides in mirth, To see old Kris in a plight like this, Toiling o'er the earth.

But alas for the Moon, he had laughed like a loon, For Kris is a hero of old, Yes, Kris is a seer; with his small reindeer, He captured the Goblins bold.

And he changed them, they say in a wonderful way, To toys, for his Christmas cheer. The big dolls stare with a goblin air, The small ones cringe with fear.

While the moonbeams prattle, I hear a rattle Of hoofs on the chimney side; Then out on the snow I gaze below, "Hurrah! it's Kris Kringle," I cried.

Then, sly as a mouse, he entered the house, And hung up his treasures so gay. Then out with a dash, he sped like a flash, Into the night, and away.

23

24